Hooray for School!
Going to School with

by Brooke Lindner
illustrated by Susan Hall

Simon Spotlight/Nick Jr.
New York   London   Toronto   Sydney

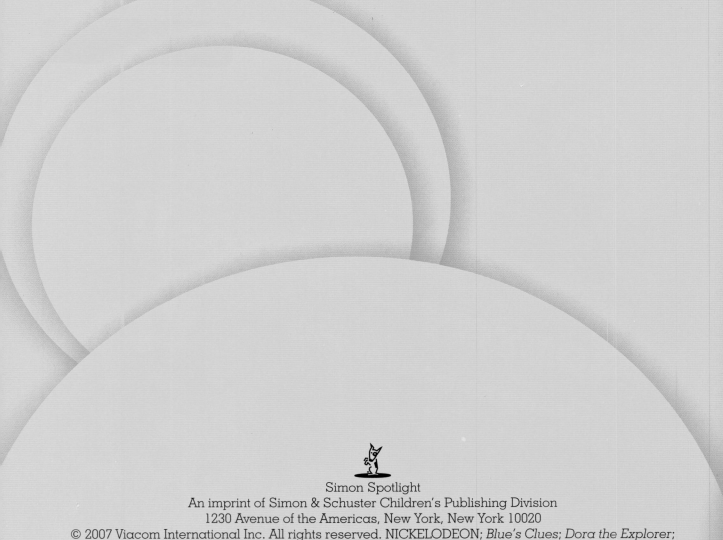

Simon Spotlight
An imprint of Simon & Schuster Children's Publishing Division
1230 Avenue of the Americas, New York, New York 10020
© 2007 Viacom International Inc. All rights reserved. NICKELODEON; *Blue's Clues; Dora the Explorer;
Go, Diego, Go!; Nick Jr. The Backyardigans;* and all related titles, logos, and characters are trademarks of
Viacom International Inc. *Blue's Clues* created by Traci Paige Johnson, Todd Kessler, and Angela C. Santomero.
All rights reserved, including the right of reproduction in whole or in part in any form.
SIMON SPOTLIGHT and colophon are registered trademarks of Simon & Schuster, Inc.
Nontoxic
Manufactured in China 1010 LEO
4 6 8 10 9 7 5
ISBN-13: 978-1-4169-5861-1
ISBN-10: 1-4169-5861-4

Tomorrow is the first day of school!
There are so many great things to
do at school.

I can't wait for school to start!
I love using the school computer.
It's just like the one I have in the
Animal Rescue Center! What do
you like to do on the computer?

I love learning new things in school. Do you know what my favorite class is? I'll give you a hint! *Uno, dos, tres, cuatro, cinco, seis, siete, ocho, nueve, diez. ¡Sí!* My favorite subject is math! What's your favorite subject?

I love seeing all of my friends at school. And I love feeding our class pet, Giggles the rabbit. What class pet would you like to have?

I like to visit the school library. I can find a lot of books about animal science there. The more I read about animals, the better I am at being an Animal Rescuer!

One of my favorite parts of school is recess! I love to play games with my friends. What are your favorite games to play at recess?

There's something else that I really love to do at school! Here's a clue: A, B, C. Yeah, I love writing letters and words, and making stories. Sometimes I even get to share my stories in class!

I can't wait for tomorrow to come!
Now it's time to go to sleep so I'll
be ready for my big day at school.
¡Buenas noches! Good night!

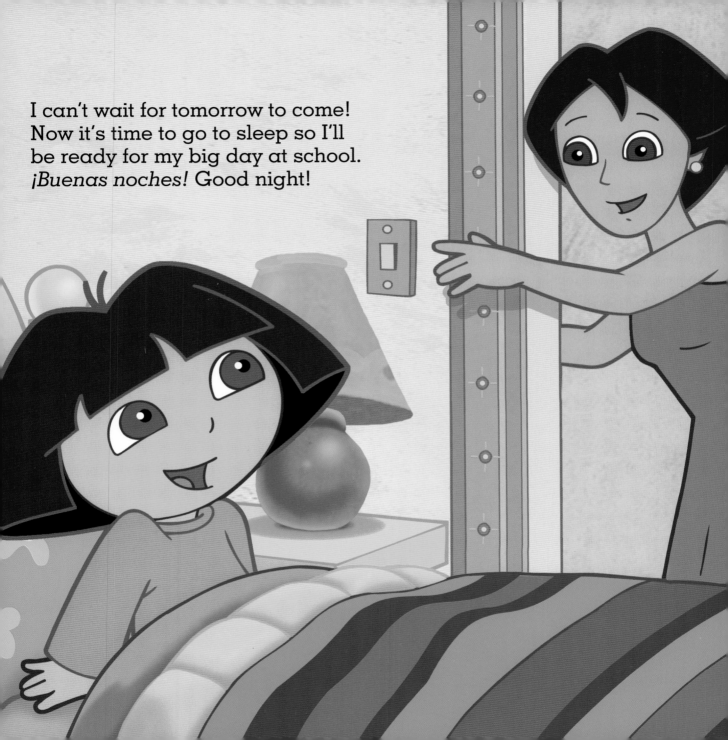

Rise and shine! It's almost time for school. Let's pack some lunch. What are your favorite foods to bring to school?

Let's check Backpack to make sure I have everything I need for school. Backpack has crayons, pencils, a notebook, a ruler, and my lunch. *¡Excelente!*

¡Vamos a la escuela!
Let's go to school!

Have a great day!